WELCOME TO
PASSPORT TO READING
A beginning reader's ticket to a brand-new world!

Every book in this program is designed to build read-along and read-alone skills, level by level, through engaging and enriching stories. As the reader turns each page, he or she will become more confident with new vocabulary, sight words, and comprehension.

These PASSPORT TO READING levels will help you choose the perfect book for every reader.

READING TOGETHER
Read short words in simple sentence structures together to begin a reader's journey.

READING OUT LOUD
Encourage developing readers to sound out words in more complex stories with simple vocabulary.

READING INDEPENDENTLY
Newly independent readers gain confidence reading more complex sentences with higher word counts.

READY TO READ MORE
Readers prepare for chapter books with fewer illustrations and longer paragraphs.

This book features sight words from the educator-supported Dolch Sight Words List. This encourages the reader to recognize commonly used vocabulary words, increasing reading speed and fluency.

For more information, please visit passporttoreadingbooks.com.

Enjoy the journey!

Little, Brown and Company

Hachette Book Group
1290 Avenue of the Americas, New York, NY 10019
Visit us at lb-kids.com

Little, Brown and Company is a division of Hachette Book Group, Inc.
The Little, Brown name and logo are trademarks of Hachette Book Group, Inc.

The publisher is not responsible for websites (or their content) that are not owned by the publisher.

First Edition: March 2014

Library of Congress Cataloging-in-Publication Data

Rosen, Lucy.
Meet Zarina the pirate fairy / by Lucy Rosen ; illustrated by the Disney Storybook Art Team. — First edition.
pages cm. — (Disney fairies) (Passport to reading. Level 1)
Based on the animated Disney movie, The pirate fairy.
ISBN 978-0-316-28330-4
I. Disney Storybook Artists. II. The pirate fairy (Motion picture) III. Title.
PZ7.R718663Mg 2014
[E]—dc23

2013042078

10 9 8 7 6 5

CW

Printed in the United States of America

Passport to Reading titles are leveled by independent reviewers applying the standards developed by Irene Fountas and Gay Su Pinnell in *Matching Books to Readers: Using Leveled Books in Guided Reading*, Heinemann, 1999.

Meet Zarina
the Pirate Fairy

By Lucy Rosen

Illustrated by the Disney Storybook Art Team

LITTLE, BROWN AND COMPANY
New York • Boston

Attention, Disney Fairies fans!
Look for these words when you read
this book. Can you spot them all?

Pixie Hollow

orange pixie dust

pirate

ship

Pixie Hollow is a magical place.

It is home to the

Never Land fairies.

The fairies have special talents.

Tinker Bell invents things.

She is a tinker fairy!

Iridessa is a light fairy.
She makes sunbeams
and rainbows!

Rosetta is a
garden fairy.
Plants bloom when
she is around.

Zarina is a dust-keeper fairy.

She helps tie up pixie dust.

Pixie dust can make things fly.

Zarina loves to learn
new things.
She asks a lot about
how pixie dust works.

It is Zarina's turn to help
work with Blue Pixie Dust.
She watches Fairy Gary
add the dust drop by drop.

Zarina dreams of creating different colors of pixie dust.

At home, Zarina tries to make
other kinds of pixie dust.

A tiny speck of
Blue Pixie Dust
falls out of her hair.

She adds it to a bowl

of regular pixie dust.

In a flash,

the dust turns orange!

"It worked!" she shouts.

Zarina invites Tinker Bell

to her house to see

the new pixie dust.

"You found orange pixie dust?"

asks Tinker Bell.

"No, Tink," says Zarina,

"I made orange pixie dust."

"That has never been done before,"

says Tinker Bell.

Zarina asks Tink to stir

another bowl.

They make purple pixie dust.

"Purple equals fast-flying

talent!" cries Zarina.

Tinker Bell is scared.

Zarina is excited.

She makes more and more

colors of dust.

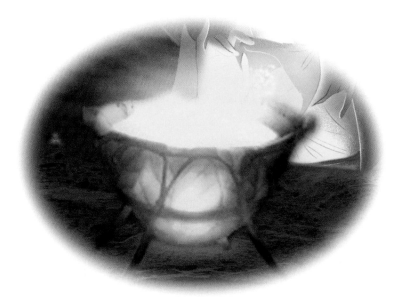

Zarina makes pink
garden-talent dust.
It spills onto a plant,
and vines grow out of
Zarina's house.

The vines grow
through Pixie Hollow.
They destroy the
Dust Depot!

Fairy Gary tells Zarina she cannot be a dust-keeper fairy. Zarina feels sad, so she flies away from Pixie Hollow.

The fairies do not see
Zarina for a long time.
She comes back
to steal the Blue Pixie Dust!
The fairies chase her.

They find Zarina on a pirate ship.

She is wearing pirate clothes.

She has new pirate friends.

Something is not right!

The fairies follow
Zarina until she
is alone.
"Why are you
doing this?"
Tinker Bell asks.

Zarina explains that she will
make pixie dust for the pirates.
"This is exactly where I belong,"
Zarina says.

"Zarina, do not do this!"

Tinker Bell cries.

"Come back home."

"I am so sorry,"

Zarina says.

She hugs her friends.

The girls take control of the
pirate ship.
They take the ship and the Blue
Pixie Dust back to Pixie Hollow.